Pussycat, Pussycat

Retold by Wes Magee
Illustrated by Beccy Blake

W

FRANKLIN WATTS
LONDON•SYDNEY

Beccy Blake

"Hello! This is me at my drawing board with my cat Molly. Molly's never been to London. She much prefers to watch all the little birds in the garden."

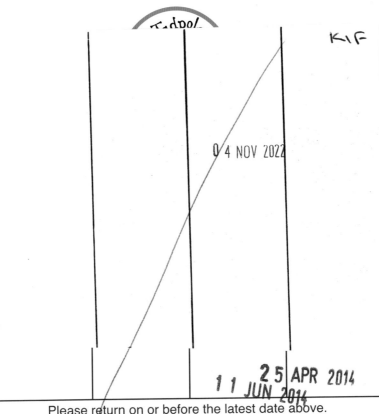

Tadpol

KIF

04 NOV 2022

25 APR 2014

1 1 JUN 2014

Please return on or before the latest date above.
You can renew online at www.kent.gov.uk/libs
or by phone 08458 247 200

1 3 SEP 2014

1 4 AUG 2017

Notes for adults

TADPOLES NURSERY RHYMES are structured to provide support for newly independent readers. The books may also be used by adults for sharing with young children.

The language of nursery rhymes is often already familiar to an emergent reader, so the opportunity to see these rhymes in print gives a highly supportive early reading experience. The alternative rhymes extend this reading experience further, and encourage children to play with language and try out their own rhymes.

If you are reading this book with a child, here are a few suggestions:

1. Make reading fun! Choose a time to read when you and the child are relaxed and have time to share the story.
2. Recite the nursery rhyme together before you start reading. What might the alternative rhyme be about? Why might the child like it?
3. Encourage the child to reread the rhyme, and to retell it in their own words, using the illustrations to remind them what has happened.
4. Point out together the rhyming words when the whole rhymes are repeated on pages 12 and 22 (developing phonological awareness will help with decoding language) and encourage the child to make up their own alternative rhymes.
5. Give praise! Remember that small mistakes need not always be corrected.

First published in 2008 by
Franklin Watts
338 Euston Road
London NW1 3BH

Franklin Watts Australia
Level 17/207 Kent Street
Sydney NSW 2000

Text (Little Bird, Little Bird)
© Wes Magee 2008
Illustration © Beccy Blake 2008

The rights of Wes Magee to be identified as the author of Little Bird, Little Bird and Beccy Blake as the illustrator of this Work have been asserted in accordance with the Copyright, Designs and Patents Act, 1988.

ISBN 978 0 7496 8033 6 (hbk)
ISBN 978 0 7496 8039 8 (pbk)

Series Editor: Jackie Hamley
Series Advisor: Dr Hilary Minns
Series Designer: Peter Scoulding

Printed in China

Franklin Watts is a division of Hachette Children's Books an Hachette Livre UK company.
www.hachettelivre.co.uk

"Pussycat, Pussycat, where have you been?"

"I've been to London
to visit the Queen!"

"Pussycat, Pussycat, what did you there?"

8

"I frightened a little mouse under her chair!"

Pussycat, Pussycat

"Pussycat, Pussycat,

where have you been?"

"I've been to London

to visit the Queen!"

"Pussycat, Pussycat,

what did you there?"

"I frightened a little mouse

under her chair!"

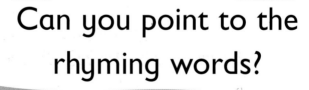

Can you point to the
rhyming words?

Little Bird, Little Bird

by Wes Magee
Illustrated by Beccy Blake

Wes Magee

"My pet cat, Rusty, is very old but she still loves to chase a furry toy mouse around the house. And she would love to meet a little bird."

"Little Bird, Little Bird, where did you fly?"

"I flew to the seaside with ships sailing by!"

"Little Bird, Little Bird, what did you see?"

19

"A crab ...

and a fish ...

and an eel for my tea!"

Little Bird, Little Bird

"Little Bird, Little Bird,

where did you fly?"

"I flew to the seaside

with ships sailing by!"

"Little Bird, Little Bird,

what did you see?"

"A crab ... and a fish ...

and an eel for my tea!"

Can you point to the
rhyming words?

Puzzle Time!

Which of these might you find at the seaside?

Answers